To: Ani

From: Aunt Kristina

YOU CAN DO IT!

a little book about the BIG POWER of PERSEVERANCE

SESAME STREET

sourcebooks jabberwocky

words by Craig Manning
pictures by Joe Mathieu

Elmo was learning to write his own name,
but the harder he tried, the worse it became!
Is it L before M, or M before L?
Elmo mixed up the letters and he just couldn't tell.

"Elmo gives up!" Elmo cried, feeling helpless and sad.
He was frustrated and also a little bit mad!
"You can do it! Don't give up!" said his mom from the door.
"With a mind made for growing, you can always learn more."

"You learned how to crawl, then you learned how to walk!
You learned how to sing once you learned how to talk.
You learned how to ride your very own trike,
and one day you'll learn how to ride a big bike!"

"It wasn't easy, but still you learned how.
You didn't give up, and look at you now!"

She's right, Elmo thought, and he knew what to do.
He'd practice and practice, then he'd write his name too!

Elmo did it! He wrote his name down nice and neat!
But how 'bout his friends around Sesame Street?
Were there things they were trying to learn how to do?
Who else could use some encouragement too?

"Skating's too hard!" Grover said with a sigh.
He sat on the curb and he started to cry!

"You can do it!" said Elmo. "With a hand from a friend, you can skate on the sidewalk from beginning to end!"

What was the Count making? Could Grover guess?
"Of course not," Count cried. "It looks like a mess!"

"You can do it!" said Grover. "Keep painting away. Practice makes perfect—you will get it someday!"

Cookie Monster loved cookies, the eating and baking,
but he struggled a lot with the counting and waiting.

"You can do it!" said Count. This is something Count knows.
"Now here's a quick tip—use your fingers and toes!"

Telly loved triangles—they were the best!
But when it came to new shapes, he forgot all the rest.

"You can do it!" said Cookie. "Me thinks you'll be great.
Just look at circles as cookies or plates!"

While playing with Rosita, Abby started to pout.
She kept dropping the ball and she wanted to shout!

"You can do it!" said Telly. "Just try not to stress.
Take in a big breath and try worrying less!"

Julia loved dancing—she spun really well.
But then she tried leaping, and whoops!—almost fell.

"You can do it!" said Abby. "You'll shine bright like the sun! You don't need to be perfect! You just need to have fun!"

Zoe was hoping to play, skip, and run,
but she couldn't keep going with her laces undone.

"You can do it!" said Julia. "You'll tie a knot and a bow!"
Keep training your fingers and you'll be a pro!

Riding a bike was Big Bird's big dream,
which is easier said than done, it would seem!

"You can do it!" said Zoe. "It's okay to fall!
Just get back up, and watch out for that wall!"

So what thing do *you* want to learn how to do?
Is it running or singing or tying your shoes?
Because if Grover can skate, and Elmo can write,
and Julia can leap in a big, bright spotlight…

If Telly learned shapes, and Abby caught a ball,
and Cookie, Count, Zoe, and Big Bird did it all…

then you're the next learner! So go on, get going!
You can **do it**, my friend! Don't ever stop growing!

Cover and internal design © 2019 by Sourcebooks, Inc.
Text by Craig Manning
Illustrations by Joe Mathieu

Sourcebooks and the colophon are registered trademarks of Sourcebooks, Inc.
All rights reserved.

Published by Sourcebooks Jabberwocky, an imprint of Sourcebooks, Inc.
P.O. Box 4410, Naperville, Illinois 60567-4410
(630) 961-3900
Fax: (630) 961-2168
sourcebooks.com

Source of Production: Shenzhen Wing King Tong Paper Products Co. Ltd.,
Shenzhen, Guangdong Province, China
Date of Production: May 2019
Run Number: 5015405

Printed and bound in China.
WKT 10 9 8 7 6 5 4 3 2